# HER MONSTROUS FATE

## A GREEK MYTHOS MONSTER ROMANCE

BRITTANY L. ADKINS

J. T. BAXTER

ISBN: 978-1-7321453-4-4

# DEDICATION

To all our readers who love a bit of naughty fun
with mythical creatures!

# CONTENTS

Acknowledgments

Letter to Our Readers

1   The King's Demand       1

2   Osteus' Disappointment       7

3   Battle for Deyanira       16

4   The Legend of Fated Mates       23

5   A Bond of Mates       32

6   A New Future       43

7   A Blessed Union       48

8   A Visit to the Shrine of Aphrodite       56

9   The Blossoming of Unions       65

10   Happiness in Fate and Monstrosity       72

# ACKNOWLEDGMENTS

To our beta readers! Thank you for loving our story and giving us feedback!

Thank you to our editor, Kala Fleming-Crowe.

To Aphrodite, thank you for blessing the union and creation of this story.

# LETTER TO OUR READERS:

Thank you so much for reading our book! You make this dream possible! If you have read Fictional Musings, you have probably read this story, but it was so incredible that it needed to be showcased. I hope you enjoy it!

I should warn you that some of the content within these pages may be triggering for some, so please read with care.

## TRIGGER WARNINGS:

Death, sex, anxiety, gore, monster sex, attempted murder, blood, sexually explicit scenes, sexual harassment, breeding, and pregnancy, there may be more, but these are the big ones.

Check the author's website if you want to see the complete list. www.witchycornerproductions.com.

## TROPES:

Star-crossed Lovers, Fated Mates, Beauty and the Beast, instalove, Monster Romance, Quick and Dirty Read, spontaneous, hero romance.

All my best,
BRITTANY & J.T.

# 1
# THE KING'S DEMAND

The village was absolutely buzzing today. The King was visiting. Many of the towns in the kingdom would see a visit from the King each year for his hunting trips. After a successful hunt, he was known for being a generous king, leaving gold in the streets. However, each town he visited was left with a strangeness, and some local maidens would go missing.

The day the king arrived, all citizens were to line

up and welcome him. Deyanira was no exception to this law. She was a young maiden of twenty-one and one of the darlings of the village. Like the other citizens, she bowed when he got off his horse and looked around at the people. He looked over each citizen as if he were searching for someone, when his gaze stopped on her. It was as if he looked her over like a prized horse at auction. A smile crept over his stern face. His smile was chilling, yet something inside her wanted to see it again. The King nodded to his man and pointed to her. Though the town was quietly awaiting their dismissal from the King, no one could hear the brief, hushed discussion between the King and his captain. With a quick nod, the captain turned and began to order his men to prepare things for the King. The King smiled and waved his hand, dismissing the townspeople.

The next afternoon, Deyanira was feeding her family's goats just outside her home when four of the king's soldiers approached her.

"Girl! His Majesty would like to see you," one said from behind the helm that covered his face.

"Me, my lord?" she replied, looking for confirmation.

"Now!" he said firmly as he grabbed her arm, making her drop the bucket of grain on the ground.

"Owww! Of course, I will go, but you don't have

to grab me!" She tried to pull from his grasp, but it was too firm.

He forced her toward the king's tent, making her stumble, but she didn't fall. As four of his heavily armored guards escorted her to the king's tent, she noticed the townspeople quickly heading into their homes as if some knew things she didn't. She was so young the last time the king visited, so she didn't remember the townspeople acting this way.

Upon arriving at the tent, the gruff guard forced her inside, making her stumble to her knees before the king. She bowed her head and then looked up at him.

"Have I done something wrong, Your Majesty?" she asked softly.

The King laughed and helped her up. "Not at all, my dear. My guards are a little rough, but they are good for protection. You aren't hurt, are you? I wouldn't want your beautiful body to be spoiled for our time together," he said as he ran his hands down over her body.

At that moment, Deyanira realized why the king had called for her. He desired her for his bed. She blushed and shook her head. "No, Your Majesty. I am unharmed. It is an honor to be here with you."

He smiled and began to circle around her. "You understand why you are here?"

She nodded. "For your bed," she said nervously.

He let out a dark laugh. "I do not fuck in my bed with common pretty things like you. I fuck in the wilds. Now go out to the woods like a good whore for me and take that dress off and wait. I will fuck you when I get there." He said as his hands groped her body.

Deyanira knew she had no choice in the matter. She nodded, pulled from his lustful grasp, and headed out to the woods. Once she stepped into the woods, she felt as if there were eyes all around her. Many hunters only ventured into the woods for hunting but never anything else. The woods were home to various creatures and monsters. She began to undress fully and looked around for him as she stood naked, waiting. Part of her did not want to be claimed by the king, but the other part was so thrilled to be chosen, and it aroused her. In truth, no one says no to the king. His temper was not one to anger.

After several dragging minutes, she heard footsteps. He had arrived.

"My, my, what a beauty you are," he said as his fingers brushed over her long brown locks.

His hands traveled down her chest to her full breasts, and his hand squeezed one softly before moving further. Her slender but voluptuous waist was his next target. Both hands grasped her sides, firmly pulling her to him.

"You are almost so perfect I wish I could keep you," he said before one hand slipped down between her full thighs. "Aroused and ready for your King. I am not yet, and I want to play a little before I take what I need. I like to chase my prey," he said in her ear. "The appropriate term would be hunt my prey. If you outrun me, you will be fucked and bred like a good village whore. If you don't...well, no one will miss you. You may have a few moments head start," he said, pushing her away as a guard appeared with a bow. "Run, little girl. Run!"

She watched him pull out an arrow and nock it in his bow before she realized he was serious. She gasped and began to run barefoot through the woods. "Help me! Please! Help me!" she screamed.

"They know better than to help you, you little bitch!" the king called after her as he shot an arrow in her direction.

She heard the arrow hit a tree. She screamed louder as she ran painfully through the forest.

# 2
# OSTEUS'
# DISAPPOINTMENT

Osteus paused with his hand on the door to the inn. He let out a soft sigh. *Was this a good idea?* He had already received several unpleasant looks as he walked into the small village. His spear was propped up against the wall of the inn. He was imposing enough without walking into a room full of people wielding a spear. He turned the handle and entered the inn, dodging immediately as a pewter jar smashed into the doorframe beside him. He looked down at the broken receptacle and then up at where it originated. The burly man behind the bar was glowering at him.

"You're not welcome here, abomination! Get out!" Osteus tightened his grip on the hilt of the sword sheathed at his belt. His nostrils flared as he surveyed the interior of the inn. A small voice in the back of his mind spoke to him. *They will revile you Osteus. Just remember, you are unique, and you deserve life.* He smiled inwardly. His mother had been a wise woman. Osteus removed his hand from the hilt of his sword and held up his palms.

"I mean no harm," he said softly. "I am simply looking for work you may have." The inn-keep kept his face stern and demanding.

"You are not wanted here," he hissed through his teeth. "Be gone!"

Osteus sighed and backed out the door, knowing better than to turn his back on any threat. Once he closed the door behind him and stepped back into the blazing midday sun, he looked around the village. He was still receiving looks from everyone there. It did not surprise him. His half-satyr, half-faun heritage lent him no favors. He was despised in every place he went. He turned south and headed for the woods.

"You! Half breed! Turn and fight!"

Osteus stopped walking and glanced over his shoulder. A group of men had gathered behind him armed with all manner of melee weapons, most of which seemed to be farming implements, though he spotted a couple of swords and daggers, too. The man who stood at the center of the group was the one who had called to him. He was large for a human, tall and heavily muscled, but still dwarfed by Osteus' height and build.

"I want no trouble," the satyr-faun called to the group. Even with the slur against his parentage, these people did not deserve harm. The man gripped an axe in his two hands.

"Too bad," he replied through gritted teeth. "You cannot come here and simply decide to take work away from honest folks." Osteus bristled. That was the second slur against him that this man had uttered in the space of as many minutes. To impeach his honor by declaring him a dishonest person was moving dangerously close to somewhere that Osteus would not walk away from.

"I do not mean to take away work from others.

I simply need to make a living, the same as all of you." He gripped his spear in his hand, his body tensing involuntarily for what he feared was to come.

"That's just it! You're nothing like us, beast!"

Osteus chuffed, expelling hot breath from his nostrils. He studied the group and watched as they all took up fighting stances. None of them seemed to have any military training, and their movements were odd and uncoordinated. He lifted his spear, turned its tip down, buried it into the ground beside him, and waited. Unsurprisingly, the group charged him as one.

Osteus braced himself as the half-a-dozen men barrelled into him, forcing him to take a step back but nothing more. He struck fast and true, his fist smashing into the nearest man's nose. Blood exploded from the broken appendage, and the man screamed, reeling backward, blood seeping through his fingers as he held his face. Osteus allowed himself a slight smirk before he felt fists pummel his torso. The hits felt nothing more than a mild annoyance, his skin tougher than that of an ordinary human. He dispatched another two of the men with a broad sweep of his arm, hitting one in the ribs and catching the other with the follow-through. They ran away from the fight, clutching their arms around their torsos, no doubt bruised and winded. Osteus did not have time to check as he was beset upon by the remaining two men who came at him with a pitchfork and a sword. He seized the hand of the man wielding the pitchfork and pushed with enough force to send the shaft of the implement back into the man's face. He cried out and tripped backward. Osteus swerved just in time to avoid the slash of the final man's sword as it came down close to his shoulder. He whirled and thrust the palm of his hand at the man's face, who swiftly dodged to the side only to find the satyr-faun's hefty goat leg swinging for his abdomen. The leg made contact with a thud as Osteus kicked the man ten feet into the nearby stone wall.

"You beast! I will make you pay for this!" roared the large man.

The man shifted his feet into a battle stance, and Osteus immediately became wary. This man had experience fighting. The way he handled the axe and his entire demeanor revealed this. Osteus kept his gaze on the man and waited for him to make the first move, but the man stood his ground, glaring at the satyr-faun before him. After what seemed like an eternity, the man screamed and ran at Osteus with the axe ready to cleave. The mighty creature dug his hooves into the earth beneath him and braced as the man performed a powerful overhead swing, attempting to cleave Osteus in two right down the middle. The movement was abruptly stopped when Osteus grabbed the man's wrists in his vice-like grasp and twisted. A shrill scream accompanied the sickening crunch of bones as the satyr-faun broke both the man's wrists in a single, swift move. The man fell to his knees, his wrists limp in his lap as he looked up at Osteus, tears in his eyes. Osteus sighed as he looked down at the man.

"Remember, I did not want this," he told the man, retrieving his upright spear from where it stuck in the ground.

He turned away from the bruised and battered, but still breathing, bodies that now littered the path and resumed his walk into the woods. The heat was making him sweat, and he needed to bathe. Heading for the pool nearest his small domicile, he watched as the village gave way to the nature of the woods.

Creatures, great and small, permeated the woods that he had called home for the past several years. The sounds and smells of nature filled his senses, and he smiled. Peaceful. It was peaceful here, away from man and their problems. He reached the pool and heard laughter coming across the wind. He could not help but smile a little more. As he pushed through the bushes, he saw them. The three water nymphs that frequented this pool sat on rocks surrounding it as they talked and laughed.

They paused as Osteus approached; their gaze wary. He could not blame them. He was a half-satyr, and satyrs did not have a good reputation with the nymphs. He slowly bowed to them, and they relaxed, motioning to the pool of water. He smiled and began to remove his weapons and armor. Moments later, he removed his clothes and set them all down within reach of the pool. Then, he slowly lowered himself into the waters. The pool was warm, heated by the midday sun and the magic of the nymphs who now sat only feet away from him. Osteus scooped water into his hands and began to wash his body. His heritage gave him a unique appearance. He retained his mother's goat legs and soft facial features, but the rest came from his father. The strong horsetail, the large, firm horns atop his head, and his dominating, untamed nature that took over him more than he liked all belonged to his father.

Osteus was nearly finished bathing when a shrill scream pierced the air. Birds exploded from nearby trees, and the nymphs dove below the water's surface, down the tunnel he knew was deep below. He climbed out of the pool and dressed quickly in his armor, strapping on his sword and picking up his spear before rushing through the woods in search of the source of the scream.

# 3
# BATTLE FOR
# DEYANIRA

Deyanira could feel cuts on her bare feet as she ran. She screamed and ducked into a thicket only to feel an arrow graze her arm. She let out a cry of pain and kept running. Exiting the thicket, she looked behind her to see the king drawing another arrow. As she turned to find a way to hide, she crashed into something large.

She looked right into the gleaming eyes of one of the woodland creatures. He looked like a satyr or a faun, but all she could do was scream and try to escape him as another arrow hit the tree next to them. She felt the creature grab her firmly but gently.

"Oh, little girl, I am growing so aroused. I think it's time to see if you bleed," he called to her. "I will find you. I always find my prey, and you will bleed for me."

Deyanira looked up at the creature that held her. She looked panicked but had no option but to hope for help.

"Help me...he is hunting me...please..." she begged in a terrified whisper.

Osteus' head snapped up from the girl who clung to him now to the band of men rushing through the woods, obviously chasing her...no, hunting her, as she said. The group stopped in their tracks as they beheld the massive satyr that stood before them, their prey clinging to it like it would save her life.

"Beast! Be gone from here!" shouted the man

who was clearly in charge of the group. He wore fine clothes and a crown. In his hand was a bow, an arrow nocked on the string. "That girl is mine!" he exclaimed.

Osteus glared at the group. He could feel the satyrian rage coursing through him. Anger, fire, bloodlust. These men would not survive their encounter with him. The powerful satyr-faun launched his spear toward the group without letting go of the girl at his side. The deadly missile hit true, skewering one of the men beside the leader and forcing him backward, pinning him to a tree. Osteus counted quickly. One down, four to go. He looked down at the girl and softly moved her arm from around him. Her arm did not even reach all the way around his body. She was small and delicate. He motioned to the tree behind him.

"Wait there," he told her, his voice gruff and commanding. She nodded slowly, her eyes still wide as she moved to the tree and leaned against it, her breath returning to her after the exhausting sprint through the woods.

Osteus unsheathed his sword from his belt, the polished iron catching the sunlight that pierced the canopy of leaves above them.

The leader of the group was red-faced as he looked back at the man Osteus had impaled to the tree.

"Fucking beast! You will die for this!" He screamed as he brought his bow up and loosed the arrow. Faster than what seemed possible for a beast of his size, Osteus deflected the arrow with his sword, his lightning reflexes taking the group aback. The leader nocked another arrow. "KILL HIM!" he shouted at his men. The other three already had their weapons out: two swords and one battle-axe. Osteus smiled as he took a fighting stance and waited. As he predicted, all three men charged him. But there was an order to their charged assault. The two with swords charged him first, coming at both his flanks while the man with the battle axe ran at him head-on.

Osteus swung his sword in a gigantic arc in front of him, catching both swordsmen with the move and instantly disemboweling them. They dropped to the ground, dead. The third man had stopped his charge before Osteus' sword came close to him, and now he stood in shock, his eyes fixated on the dead bodies of his comrades. Osteus flicked his sword, blood from the two dead men splattering to the ground. He then turned his attention to the man with the battle axe.

"I will give you *one* chance to live," he said, his eyes boring into the man's. "Drop your weapon and leave…or die." The man visibly paled, but his grip tightened on his axe. Osteus raised an eyebrow. Brave man. Foolish, but courageous. The axe-wielding man screamed a war cry and swung his weapon at the satyr-faun. Osteus dropped to one knee, the blow swinging clear over his head as he thrust forward his sword, impaling the man through the chest. The crack of the man's ribs as the sword broke them was audible, and he coughed once, blood bubbling from his mouth. Osteus retracted his blade, and the man collapsed beside his two comrades. Only then did Osteus become aware of the arrow protruding from his left arm. He looked back to the leader, who was frantically searching for another arrow in his quiver. Osteus roared, an almighty beastly sound, and the man shot his gaze back to the satyr. Then, unexpectedly, he turned and ran. He ran so fast that Osteus thought Hermes himself was carrying him. Osteus watched until he was out of sight and then laughed, snapping the arrow, leaving just a small section lodged in his arm. He would deal with that later. The grass near him rustled, and he turned to see the girl, no…the young woman, walking gingerly toward him. He wiped his sword off on one of the fallen men's tunics and then sheathed the weapon, holding up his hands to her.

"Do not fear me," he said in his commanding voice.

She nodded as she stepped closer. It was then that his nostrils filled with the smell of more blood, and he looked down. Her feet were bare and bleeding. His eyes slowly moved up her body. She was bare everywhere. He sighed and took a step closer to her. She looked like she was about to step back but stood firm. Surprisingly, she allowed him to take her into his arms, and he cradled her against his chest, her wounded feet hanging over one of his arms. Then he turned and headed back to the pool.

# 4

# The Legend of Fated Mates

Deyanira clung to the beast so tightly she was sure she was hurting him. She let out a soft sob as she realized she was safe. At least safer than when she was running from the King. She buried her face against him, terrified to let go.

Soon, she felt him lean down and sit her carefully on the bank of a pool. It took her a moment to loosen her grip on him.

"I know I shouldn't trust you, but please…don't leave me?" she said, looking up at him. Her voice was hoarse from her screams and still riddled with fear.

She felt hands gently grasp her ankles, making her jump and gasp. She looked down to see two nymphs gently pulling her into the water.

"We won't hurt you. Let us help," one of the nymphs said in a gentle and soothing voice.

"You…won't? Don't you steal humans?"

The two nymphs giggled. "No, that's a silly myth made by humans. We will help you."

The nymphs gently guided Deyanira into the water and began to clean her body with gentleness. One nymph stepped out of the forest and placed a flower crown of roses, black lilies, and calla lilies on her head. The nymph smiled warmly at her.

"We understand men's deplorable nature. You are safe here amongst the monsters, beasts, and mythical creatures, as you humans call us," the forest nymph told her before returning to the trees.

Deyanira was astonished at the welcoming nature of this place and these creatures. Humans would have never been this kind to her. Her attention was brought back to the sizeable satyr-like creature. There was something about him. Something that made her desire to remain near him. She didn't understand why she didn't want to leave his side. Her instincts told her to run, but the very thought made her want to cry as if her heart was breaking. She met his eyes. They were gentle despite the horror she had just witnessed at his hands.

"Thank you. I can never repay what you did. But I also know I can never go back. The King will have me killed." She tried to stifle a sob, but it was no use. Her tears flowed freely.

Osteus sighed as he knelt beside her. He winced as the adrenaline in his system started to wear off, and he felt the throbbing in his arm where the arrow shaft was still lodged.

"You have nothing to fear here," he told the young woman. "I am sorry you had to witness what happened back there, but those men deserved nothing less than death." He began to remove his armor, the bronze chest plate that covered his torso, stylized as if it had muscles of its own. When he removed it, his body had the same muscles as the armor. He wore no greaves or sandals, his goat legs offering more than enough protection. All that was left was his waistband, the strips of cloth covered with leather tassets that protected his nether regions. He suddenly became painfully aware that the woman in front of him was naked, and the sight of her now in this peaceful situation made his

25

arousal grow. He felt himself harden beneath his waistband, but he could do nothing about it. He had to get into the pool to clean his wound and the grime of the battle from his body. He sighed and removed the waistband, his cock springing free as he did so. This was another characteristic of his father's side. Although his mixed heritage meant he was not in a permanent state of erectness like all other male satyrs, he had inherited the enlargement common to them. He sank into the water, thankful it was still warm, and slowly worked on healing his wounded arm. It then dawned on him that he had no idea who this woman was or why she was being chased.

"What is your name?" he asked her gently. "And why were those men chasing you?"

Deyanira blushed, seeing how handsome his body was. She also noticed how his body responded to what she could only assume was her nakedness, making her blush deeper.

"The King takes women as lovers from each village he visits on his hunts. Now...I realize why his lovers have not returned. It was presumed he took them home...no, he kills them. He wanted me to be his prey, as he called it," she replied as she felt the nymphs continue to clean the scratches and wounds on the rest of her body. "I am Deyanira...my name is Deyanira. What is yours?

Also, what do you plan to do with me?" she asked as the nymphs guided her deeper into the pool closer to him.

"My name is Osteus," he replied gruffly, seeming momentarily lost in thought. "And I have no plans to do anything with you. You screamed for help, and I helped."

Deyanira knew the legends and knew Fauns were kind and lustful but not as lascivious as Satyrs. Satyrs could be cruel and fearsome, and their lust knew little boundaries. Yet here he was, and he was her savior. He looked like a mixture of the two.

As her eyes traveled over his body, they stopped at the arrow he had taken for her. Her small hand gently touched the wood still protruding from his arm. It was a delicate touch.

"I can help remove this if you will allow me. It is my fault you have it," she said in her almost hoarse whisper.

He felt her hand on his arm and paused, looking down at her as she sat next to him in the pool, and watched as the nymphs cleaned her wounds. The warmth of her hand on his arm was…pleasant. It had been a long time since he had been touched by anyone. He realized he had been staring at her and had not answered her.

"I would appreciate your help," he told her.

He spoke as she started to work on removing the arrow from his arm.

"What your king did, there is no honor in that. A man with such power should not be allowed to abuse it." He winced as she pulled the arrow from his arm, and blood started to flow freely into the pool.

He wrapped a bandage from his pack around his arm, tight enough to staunch the flow of blood. It was then he caught her glancing at his hardened cock beneath the water. He felt himself stir, and he smirked a little. His blood began to boil, not with anger, but with arousal. The primal nature of the satyr and the softer side of the faun in him fighting for dominance. His eyes roved over her body. Her full breasts were large for her slender form, but her waist and hips were curved, making her entire body a beautiful sight to behold. His cock twitched in the water, and he saw her cheeks redden as she noticed the movement.

She had an overwhelming desire to be close to him. She felt her hands slip up his chest as she stood before him. Her eyes traveled up until they met his. She slowly pulled her hands away from his body as she realized how intimate she was getting with him.

"Is this some sort of satyr magick? I have this overwhelming feeling of being close to you. I should be afraid of you…all the legends of your kind say you are not safe for humans. But I don't want to leave your side…" she said, clasping her hands together so she wouldn't give in to her desires.

He looked at her with concern despite his burning need to take her.

"There is no magick at work here, at least…not any that I am doing willingly. But I also have this desire, more so than just to have you…but to be yours and claim you." He paused as he felt himself twitch again. Then it hit him.

"There is a legend of fated mates," he told her softly. "A bond so powerful that it transcends all others. Could that be what this is?" he asked out loud, more so to himself than to her. He moved his hands slowly and rested them on her waist. His hands were so massive that he could wrap them around her entire waist if he wanted to. *Could they truly be fated mates?* Him, a satyr and faun hybrid, and her, a human. His eyes moved from hers down to what lay between her thighs. It didn't even seem possible that he could fit inside her. The thought burned through him, and he shook his head.

She felt his hands on her waist. His touch was like oxygen to a flame. She needed more. Her hands returned to his chest as she hesitantly let them slip over his shoulders.

"I have heard those stories, but I always assumed they weren't real..." she began as she felt him pull her closer to him. "Osteus..." she said his name almost as a moan as she felt her breasts press against his chest. "How do we know for sure?" she asked as she licked her lips.

The fear was gone from her body, and the pain was fleeting from the warm, soothing waters. But her arousal and desire to be his were growing rapidly. She couldn't understand how this creature, whom many would call a monster, longed to be hers.

# 5
# THE BOND OF MATES

His name on her lips was like nectar from the Gods, and he moaned softly as she pressed her breasts against his chest. He could feel her nipples pebbled against his muscles, making his cock ache for her. He looked into her eyes.

"I think the fact that you're so ready, so willing to be close to me, even though all logic says you should stay away, is proof enough," he told her. "There is something, some force, making us feel this way. There has to be." He moved his hands down and cupped her ass, slowly lowering her to sit in his lap. He groaned as he felt her soft folds rub down his shaft. She was wet, so very wet, and not from the waters of the pool. He gritted his teeth as he felt his lust taking over. All he wanted was to impale her on his cock right there and then, but he didn't want to hurt her. He wanted her to be his, in every sensual and feral way possible, but he would never hurt her purposefully...at least, not unless she asked him to. His head swam with the thoughts, and before he knew what he was doing, his lips were on hers. The kiss was hard and passionate, but also caring and meaningful. She would not be just a fuck to him. She was meant for him. This he knew down to his very core.

"Deyanira..." he moaned into their kiss.

Lust and desire filled her body as if his kiss was the spark that started the wildfire between them. She wrapped her arms around him as much as she could as the feeling of his thick cock pressed against her folds. Hearing him say her name was like hearing Aphrodite's blessing of their union.

"Please Osteus...I want to be yours, please..." she begged against his lips.

She could feel his strong hands grasp her body and gently begin to guide her down on his cock.

Osteus groaned with pleasure. The tip of his

cock found her entrance. He cursed inwardly, knowing he was too big for her. The satyr heritage was a curse in this sense. He looked into her eyes.

"Deyanira…this…this might hurt at first," he told her.

She caressed his cheek and nodded as she kissed him back. He felt her tongue brush his, and he tightened his grip on her body ever so slightly as he pushed her down onto his cock. He moaned into their kiss, and he heard her gasp in pain. He paused, but she smiled and nodded, a silent plea for him to continue. He did so. Her pussy was so tight, so very, very tight around the thickness of his cock, that he was afraid he was going to hurt her. But then he heard her moans. He felt her wetness coat his cock as she enveloped him, and he growled. And unexpectedly, he was there, at the very bottom of her. He had filled her all the way to the entrance to her womb, his cock buried inside her like they were meant to fit together. The feeling was beyond words.

"Fuuuuck," was all that escaped his lips as his head rolled backward, feeling her tight wetness surround him. "You feel incredible," he told her, his breath catching with every minute movement either of them made.

She knew it would hurt, but Gods above, she would have given her soul to Hades to feel him in her like this. She would desire to feel him like this for the rest of her days.

She let out a loud, lustful moan as she rolled her hips slowly. The pleasure was almost overwhelming. She buried her face against his neck as she felt his hands guiding her in a slow and intimate rhythm. She held onto him tightly as they claimed each other.

Each slow movement was like entering Olympus and torture all at the same time for them. Osteus gripped her luscious hips tightly, trying to hold back the satyrian lust coursing through him like wildfire.

"I know you are trying to be kind and gentle for me, but I can feel the struggle within you...I don't know how, but I can. I trust you. Claim me how you need. I give you permission...my mate..." the word mate rolled off her tongue like she had said it a million times before. She kissed him again, feeling like a tether had formed between them. She could feel his desire, his longing for her, and dare she say, his love.

Osteus' eyes widened at her words. His breath caught, and he growled deeply in his throat. This woman had just offered herself to him, had called him her mate, and told him to claim her. He didn't want to hurt her, but he knew he needed to claim her as his. He looked into her eyes, put his hand to her cheek, and smiled.

"You are mine, Deyanira," he growled, and then, he took her. He wrapped his hands around her waist, holding her before he started to bounce her on his cock, not slow and delicately, but fast and deep, every movement forcing his cock to fill her again and again. He cursed as his breath hitched.

"By the gods!" he exclaimed as he felt her pussy grip his cock every time he entered her. She was moaning loudly now, the woods filled with the sounds of their ecstasy. The nymphs had long departed the pool, and even the wildlife around them seemed to be keeping a distance away, respecting the sanctity of their union.

His cock throbbed inside her, and his heart beat faster and faster. It had been years since he'd had any woman, never mind one as beautiful as the one he held in his hands now. He moved out of the water, his cock still buried inside her, and sat down on the bank at the edge of the pool. Now, he could feel her wetness dripping down his shaft as she bounced on it repeatedly. The feeling of her around him was something he never wanted to let go of. Then he felt it, the surge in his balls, the warning that orgasm was close. He held onto her, his grip tightening as he looked into her eyes. She met his eyes, and they both knew what was happening. She nodded to him.

"Do it, Osteus, breed me, my mate!"

He lost all control. He roared as his orgasm ripped through him, and he thrust up into her while bringing her down on him. The tip of his cock pressed against her womb, and cum exploded from his cock, his balls pumping and pumping the hot, thick liquid into her waiting womb. His entire body tensed as the orgasm took hold of him, and he became keenly aware that so much of his cum was leaking out of her, down his cock and balls, and onto the ground beneath them.

She hadn't stopped. She couldn't. She wasn't ready to come, not yet. She desired to feel him just a moment longer. She continued to bounce hard on his cock as she felt her pussy begin to tighten around his thick cock. She tossed her head back in pleasure as she grabbed his horns for leverage as she rode him hard. Her moans and cries of pleasure could be heard at a distance as she felt her orgasm explode, drenching his cock in her juices.

Her pace began to slow after a few moments, only for her to see him smiling wickedly at her. She blushed and leaned in to kiss him, only to feel his hand slip around her throat.

"Not yet, my love. First, I must hear those cries again." He said, lifting her off his cock and laying her on the soft moss of the bank, and moving down between her thighs. "I need to taste what is mine and only mine."

Deyanira blushed and spread her legs wide for him, presenting herself to him fully. She would give him the world if she could, but for now, she would give herself to him. She watched as he grasped her legs and pulled her up to his awaiting lips.

His eyes met hers as he placed a soft kiss on her mound. "When I am finished, every creature in Greece will know you belong to me."

He felt her pulse against his lips as he kissed her again, and then, he opened his mouth and ran his strong tongue down her slit, parting her folds with the muscle as he went down. The moan from her was loud, and he felt it through her entire body. Osteus smiled at her response to his tongue, and slowly, he teased her, stroking it up and down her folds, parting them ever so slightly, and pushing the tip into her entrance before withdrawing it. He noticed the small button above her mound quivering, and a wicked grin crossed his face. He closed his mouth over her clit and sucked once before using his tongue to circle it, flicking and feeling her buck slightly at the sensation. He held her legs down, his strength pinning her to the ground, unable to move, entirely at his mercy. He moaned against her clit, the vibration causing her to buck more before he took his mouth off her and looked into her eyes.

"Mine, all mine," he growled as he plunged his tongue inside her dripping cunt. She screamed, and he paused for a second before realizing it was a scream of pleasure as his tongue stretched her. Admittedly it was not as big a stretch as his cock had been, but the feeling was undoubtedly intense for her. His tongue was by far more muscular and firmer than a human's. He guessed to her it would feel almost like a human cock. She moaned loudly as he swirled his tongue inside her, tasting her insides for the first time and realizing the taste on his tongue was a mixture of both their orgasms. Combined, they were sweet—definitely the nectar of the Gods.

There was no stopping him, nor did she want him to. His tongue was something the Gods must have spent ages perfecting. She reached down and grasped his horns, pulling him deeper into her. Her legs were locked in his tight grasp. It would have been impossible to escape him, not that she ever wanted to.

"Great Gods! Osteus! Do not stop!" she cried to the heavens as he continued devouring her like his last meal.

A low, rumbling growl escaped his lips as he looked up at her, and his grip tightened almost painfully on her thighs. He had no intentions of stopping until he was covered in her juices like a proud warrior covered in blood. His tongue penetrated her deeply, driving her wild with every thrust. As her pussy tightened around him, he knew it wouldn't be long until he would have his desire.

Deyanira screamed out as she bucked against him. Her orgasm burst free from her with a force she had never known, making her shudder in his hands. She felt him pull his tongue back and lap up every savory drop of her gently, allowing her to come down from the heavens. He chuckled as she finally let go of his horns and allowed him to look at his mate in all her spent glory.

"You are the most beautiful creature I have ever laid my eyes upon. I don't know if I have ever felt love before for anyone outside of my family, but for you, my sweet little lamb, I dare say I love you," he proclaimed.

Deyanira blushed as she panted still from the beastly orgasm he had just given her. "I love you too. It feels as if I have loved you forever."

Osteus smiled as he let go of her thighs and slowly leaned down to kiss her. Their lips met, and the kiss was soft and loving. He carefully picked her up from the ground and carried her back into the pool, this time to wash the aftermath of their sex away. He softly and caringly cleaned her as they sat together in the pool. It was early evening now. They had been at the pool for longer than he had thought, but the water remained warm, no doubt thanks to the nymphs.

# 6
# A NEW FUTURE

After several minutes of cleaning, the pair got out of the pool. Osteus began to dress in his clothes and armor and then became painfully aware that Deyanira had no clothes. She had left them behind in the woods when the king had ordered her to remove them. He sighed softly and picked her up in his arms.

"I'm going to take you back to my home. I may have some clothes you can wear, and we can figure out what happens now," he told her. She nodded as she lay in his arms, grateful he had opted to carry her as her feet, while healing from the nymph's ministrations, still stung from the cuts she had sustained while being chased.

Not long after they left the pool, they entered a small clearing deeper into the woods. There, a small hut constructed of wood and stone stood. On one side of the hut, there was a small garden, and on the other side, what looked like a small blade-sharpening wheel was tucked under an awning.

Osteus shouldered open the door and walked inside carrying Deyanira. The inside was sparse but cozy. A small fireplace was set into one wall, embers charring the last pieces of wood. A bed large enough to hold a beast of Osteus' size was against another wall. He carried her to the bed and sat her down gently before rummaging through a pile of clothes at the foot of the bed. He pulled out a large shirt and sniffed it quickly before handing it to her. She gratefully accepted it and pulled it over her naked body, shivering slightly. He looked back at the fire and proceeded to add more logs to it, stoking it with the iron poker at the side. The fire roared to life in minutes, and he remained there, hunched over it, his goat legs supporting his massive frame.

Deyanira scooted off the bed and came to sit beside him on a stool near the fire. She held her hands out to feel the fire, and it was not long before the warmth filled the hut.

She finally looked up at him. "My love…what will happen now? I have never dreamed of being someone's love, let alone someone's fated mate. Most humans marry for money, land, or titles. It is rare to marry for love. It seems I'm saying it out loud and feeling how I feel towards you… Humans may be more of the monsters than the beasts of the land."

Osteus listened to his mate before getting down to her level. "My little lamb. Some humans are evil. Your King is one. But…here you are, the lady of our home. I will protect you and love you so fiercely that Hades will question if it is the right choice to take you on the day when you pass from my arms. But until that day, I will give you all of me. You are home and safe. Everything else is just small details we will work out," he said before reaching up and caressing her cheek with his strong hand.

Deyanira leaned forward and kissed her mate with all the love within her.

# 7
# A BLESSED UNION

In the weeks after Deyanira's arrival, the two spent each moment talking and getting to know one another. Each conversation led them to a deeper understanding of who they were and how much they truly were meant for one another.

Osteus felt a strong desire to be a valiant provider for his mate now. Before, he had only ever been responsible for himself, but now he was

Deyanira's protector and love.

With a new morn and the arrival of Helios, the god of the sun, he knew he must leave his beloved in search of work. He gathered his gear and weapons and softly kissed her on the forehead before leaving their peaceful home and heading toward one of the nearby villages.

Later that evening, he wandered back through the door to their home. His tunic was bloodied and torn, and he had several wounds from swords and spears.

"My love?" Deyanira rushed to him and brought him to sit down by the fire. "What happened?" she asked as she looked him over and then set to cleaning and bandaging his wounds quickly.

"Men..." Osteus sighed and then let out a growl as she cleaned one of his wounds.

"I am sorry. Why did they attack you?" she asked as she lightened her touch, making sure to clean the wounds thoroughly.

He reached up and softly touched her arm, silently asking for forgiveness for his growl. When she smiled at him, he knew there was no darkness between them. He breathed deeply, allowing his mate to continue to care for him.

"Because I am not a human, and they view me as a monster." He answered, feeling defeated.

Deyanira put down the cloth and dried her hands before turning him to look into her eyes. "You are not a monster. You were born a mythical creature by the hands of the Gods. You are mated to a human. That was no accident of The Fates, my love. We are blessed, and tomorrow, I will be going with you to show them exactly how you are to be treated. You are a worthy ally and friend. They should cherish you for that, not fear you.

Osteus silently thanked the Gods and Fates for bringing him such a beautiful and fiercely loyal woman. Never in all his years had he imagined a woman like her would be his mate.

Hours later, she had finished tending to his wounds and ensuring they ate after their long day.

"My love?" she asked.

"Yes, my lamb?" he replied, putting down his tankard to give her his full attention.

"Do you know if we could ever have children?" she asked him curiously.

He was quiet for a moment. "Yes, I believe so. Do you believe you are with child?" he asked excitedly.

She smiled. "I do not as of yet, but as much as we make love. I am hopeful. I would love to be blessed with our children. I have always dreamed of being a mother."

Osteus stood and quickly scooped her up into his arms. "Then we shall make it so. May Aphrodite bless our union and grant us many children!" He beamed with excitement, half in declaration and half in prayer.

She giggled as he quickly undressed her and laid her down in their bed. "I did not realize how excited you would be by my question."

He then began to untie the ties on his waistband and remove them so he was unhindered to make love to his mate. He moved over her, running his tongue up her abdomen until his lips found hers. One look at her naked form and the satyrian side of him was longing to be free to claim his mate over and over again with unbridled lust.

Deyanira let out a soft gasp before her lips claimed his. His very touch was enough to ignite a flame of desire in her that burned brighter than the braziers of Olympus. She spread her legs slowly beneath him, allowing his length to brush against her freely.

Osteus growled softly into their kiss as he felt his cock brush against her wet folds. He took hold of himself and slowly moved his tip to her entrance, nudging against it gently. He looked into her eyes and kissed her deeply as he pushed inside her, her pussy stretching around his thickness and enveloping him in warmth. He moaned as he pressed as far as he could inside her until the head of his cock touched her cervix. He growled again in pleasure.

Her moans filled the small hut as they became intertwined with each other. Osteus' deep, slow thrusts were enough to drive her mad with lust and longing. They both longed to savor their love until desires could no longer be held back, and their primal passions consumed them both.

His large, strong hands ran over her body, gripping her rougher until he found her wrists and pinned them above her head with one hand. He looked down into his mate's eyes and began to thrust deep and hard into her. He loved watching her face as she melted into his embrace. His sweet little lamb was always willing to fulfill any need and desire he had, but now he only had one. He needed to breed her and needed to ensure she would be filled with his child.

He let go of her wrists and ran his hands down her small frame as he grasped her hips. His eyes were transfixed on her belly as he thrust faster into her. He could hardly wait to watch her belly swell with time. It aroused him to no end.

"By the Gods, my lamb…You will make the most beautiful mother," he growled as he listened to the beautiful symphony of her moans and his hard thrusts into her soaked folds.

Deyanira smiled between her lustful moans of divine pleasure. "I only can hope, my love… please Osteus…Don't stop!" she cried out as he was sending her close to her climax.

Osteus had no intention of stopping until they both were satisfied and she was filled. If her desire was to be a mother, he would stop at nothing to make her dream come true. Her happiness was his everything.

He reached down and softly cupped her cheek in his hand. "Look at me, my love. Look at me while I fill you, and if the Gods are kind, you will be made a mother on this day. Oh…Deyanira!" He thrust one final time into her as his seed flooded into her like a torrent.

She looked up into her mate's eyes as her body quivered with her orgasmic peak. A scream of pleasure expelled her lungs as she felt Osteus begin to satisfy her.

Soon, he withdrew from her and pulled her against him protectively as they both began to descend from their climactic highs. He softly ran his hands over her body, being sure to massage all the points where he had roughly held her during their session. He softly kissed and smiled down at her, only to see her looking up at him with love. He was blessed.

# 8

# A VISIT TO THE SHRINE OF APHRODITE

The next morning, Deyanira woke before him and gathered some flowers and herbs for tea to prepare breakfast while she allowed her mate to sleep. She was happier than she had ever been in all of her days. She only hoped that her being a human would help him and not hinder him in terms of working alongside other humans.

She soon heard the floorboards creak behind her under Osteus' large frame. She smiled as she felt his large hand slip around her waist and pull her against him gently.

"Good morning, my lamb. You didn't wake me at sunrise?" he said as he softly kissed her neck.

She closed her eyes and savored his kisses. "I figured you could use the rest after your battle yesterday… and our lovemaking." she said with a soft giggle.

Osteus also let out a soft chuckle. "That is true. I was quite exhausted after we finished." He let her go so she could continue to prepare their breakfast.

He walked around to the table near the kitchen, sat down, and watched her. He was honored with how much she loved to take care of him and their home in just a few short weeks together. Weeks that had come to feel more like precious years.

"My lamb? Do you believe it is wise for you to come with me today?" he asked with concern in his voice.

"Osteus, if I have learned anything from being your mate, it is that we are stronger together. I know what it was to be meek, and I now wish to be strong for you," she said as she sat a plate of food and a cup of tea before him.

He couldn't do anything except chuckle. His little lamb was not as weak as she was when he had found her. It was as if the strength of his mythos was beginning to imprint upon her. He was now learning it was better not to fight against her.

She sat beside him as they ate and prepared for their journey.

A couple of hours later, they entered the small town, which was bustling with life. They both walked through the town and soon found the local tavern. She walked in with him and pulled her cloak hood back. As soon as he did the same, several men stood up and grabbed their weapons.

"Be calm, friends! He is not a monster. He is a friend…an ally. I can promise you this." She exclaimed, stepping in front of Osteus protectively.

"Why would you defend this beast, woman?" One of the men called out to her.

She felt Osteus shift his hooves behind her. He was armed with his weapons, and with his stature, he towered imposingly over any man. She held her hand behind her, pressing her palm to his abdomen.

"Because he is my mate, but furthermore, he saved me from being hunted by men. If it were not for him, I would have been raped and killed." She explained to the entirety of the tavern.

"Hunted? You... you are a survivor of the King of Athens, aren't you?" a middle-aged man said, walking up to her.

Deyanira looked at him and stepped back closer to Osteus. Concern and dread filled her as she worried that this may be an ally of the King. She simply nodded.

The man put his hand on her upper arm. "My daughter... she made it back to our village... she died two days later in our home," the man explained solemnly.

The other men still holding their weapons tightly, looked at Osteus, before one spoke. "Is what she says true, monster?"

Deyanira looked at the man. "Do not call him that! Or I will be the one to rip your tongue from your mouth!" she said with a biting venom. Osteus put his hand on her hip protectively.

The victim's father held up his hand. "You will treat them with respect. If you ask again with respect, Jakar, he may answer you."

Osteus' gaze turned to Jakar as he awaited to

see what the man would do.

"My… apologies. Is what the woman says true?" Jakar asked again.

Osteus nodded. "Every word. When I found her, or rather when she ran into me, she was bloody and naked, and the king and his men were chasing her. The king fled before I could put my spear through him. The rest of his men were not so fortunate. I knew she couldn't return to her village, and the more I cared for her, the more our bond grew. She is my mate, my fated mate. I mean no harm to her or any other humans, but I will defend myself and her if necessary."

The tavern grew eerily quiet. It was clear that they had known of the king's betrayal of his people, but now, to hear it again firsthand was gut-wrenching.

The victim's father looked at Osteus. "What can we do for you?"

Osteus looked shocked and shook his head to regain his composure. "I would like work. Honest work. I am sure there is much that your village needs aid with, and I am happy to help where I can for pay or supplies."

The men nodded, returning their weapons to their sheaths or resting places as the tavern keeper approached them and handed them a parchment. "Here is a list of jobs that we need help with.

Honest work for honest pay."

Osteus smiled as he looked down at his mate, smiling happily. "Thank you."

The victim's father looked at them. "I am Niko, the mayor of this town. You are most welcome. Ma'am, if you see our shopkeeper, tell her I sent you and get what supplies you need. No harm will ever befall either of you here. Welcome to Meece," he said to them both.

Deyanira looked at Osteus. "I will gather supplies and visit the God's shrine while you work."

Osteus kissed her lovingly. "Be safe, my love." He then headed out to do one of the jobs on the list as she headed to the shop.

Once Deyanira had finished gathering what they needed and packing it into a cart that had been a gift from one of the families, she headed to the Shrine of Aphrodite at one of the sacred pools on the outskirts of the town. Along the way, she gathered wild roses and lilies to give as an offering to the goddess.

Once she arrived at the sacred pool, she heard giggles of laughter as she saw a couple of nymphs duck away out of sight. She smiled and began to clear away any plant debris from the shrine. Once she was finished, she laid down her offering and said her prayers to the great Goddess, hoping for a blessed union and many healthy children with her mate.

As she prayed, she soon heard a twig snap behind her, making her jump slightly. She quickly turned to see Osteus walking up behind her.

"Apologies, my lamb. I was trying not to startle you. I seem to have failed, though," he said with a soft smile.

She was relieved it was only him. "It's quite all right, my love. I was finishing my prayers and offerings."

She stood, brushed herself off, and then grabbed the handle of the cart when Osteus stopped her.

"No, my love, I will get this," he said warmly. You got us quite a bounty here," he said as they ventured back into the woods toward their home.

"The shopkeeper insisted. She also placed her hand on my belly and said we would need more to come. I thought it strange, but sometimes the wise women know things," she replied as they walked deeper into the twilight-darkening woods.

"Did you tell her anything about our efforts for trying for a child?" he asked curiously.

Deyanira shook her head. "Not a word."

Osteus smiled and turned to her to kiss her but stopped and sniffed the air. "We aren't alone."

# 9
# The Blossoming of Unions

Osteus pulled Deyanira down next to the cart to shield her. He grabbed his sword and unsheathed it from his belt. Soon, a man emerged from behind a tree holding a great ax. Osteus knew this man. He was one of the men who attacked him in the other village.

"I have been hunting you since you left my

brother for dead, beast! I will cut you down like a tree and leave you to bleed as I take your woman!" the man exclaimed.

Deyanira looked at the man from behind the cart as Osteus took a battle stance.

"You will not touch her!" Osteus roared as he charged towards the man with sheer rage.

Before he knew what was happening, the only slightly smaller than Osteus man had sidestepped the large satyr-faun.

The man with the ax swung, trying to bring the ax down on Osteus' back, but missed as Osteus rolled clear of the swing.

Back on his hooves, Osteus raised his sword in a defensive stance.

"A shame, beast! We could have ended this quickly. Tell me, does your woman scream when she comes?" the man teased with a wicked smirk.

Osteus saw red and chuffed, hot breath blowing out his nostrils. He raised his sword and charged the man again. Too late did he see the trap that had been laid. With the speed his powerful goat legs gave him, Osteus was not the quickest to change direction mid-charge. The man swung his ax into the ground at Osteus' hooves.

Deyanira watched the two battle as if they were almost equals. Fear filled her. She couldn't sit back and watch as this monstrous human tried to murder her mate for just being a mythic creature. She saw Osteus fall back, and before he could get up, the man was about to swing his ax down, but he stopped, and soon, blood began to pour out of his mouth as a spear tip was thrust through the front of his throat. Osteus watched as his mate pushed his spear through the back of the man's neck, blood pouring from the wound. The man coughed, blood spattering onto Osteus' chest. He quickly stood and watched the man fall to the ground.

"My lamb…" he said softly as he looked over at her.

"I couldn't let him hurt you…" she said softly as her body still shook with adrenaline.

Osteus grabbed her and pulled her into him tightly. "You did wonderfully. That took bravery. Most would have frozen in your place. You didn't. I am proud of you. My lamb is now a warrior," he said proudly.

"You are not upset?" she said softly.

Osteus cupped her face in his hands. "I am far from upset. I am proud… in love… grateful… and even aroused."

She blushed. "You are aroused?"

He let out a deep laugh. "Yes. First blood, as it is called in my world, is often brought on before a need to… make love to someone. So yes, I am aroused."

She felt the fear wane into a shared excitement with him. "And I am assuming you cannot wait until we are home?"

Osteus smiled a wicked smile. "No, I cannot. I need my mate now."

She smiled, and it was the only thing he needed from her. He grabbed her, pulled off her dress quickly, and took off his waistband freeing his raging cock. He then picked her up, so she was facing away from him, her eyes on those of the statue of Aphrodite in the shrine, slipped her down on his cock, and began to take her very roughly. If anyone was watching them, they would see her legs spread wide and her body on display as he thrust hard and deep into her.

Osteus had no desire to be gentle at this moment. This was a need for lust, and the satyr in him was fully in control of this moment. He relished her loud moans and cries of pleasure. They were like the sweetest song of the muses in his ears.

Deyanira was at his mercy, but she loved every moment of it. "Turn me to face you, my mate. I need to look into your eyes. Please?" she begged.

Osteus was happy to oblige. He quickly lifted her and turned her around, so she was now facing him before his cock was back inside her. He let out a loud growl as he gripped her thighs so tightly, she thought they might bruise, but it would be worth it.

She reached up and grasped his horns and began to use them for leverage to take him harder and faster. They were both consumed in a frenzy of desire and lust that was so strong the Gods themselves would blush at their union.

Osteus growled as she grabbed his horns. "Yes! That's it, my mate! Take it and scream in honor of Aphrodite and her perfect union between us!" he exclaimed as he watched her embrace the lust and pleasure.

She let out unbridled cries of pleasure in honor of Aphrodite. Each thrust drove her wilder than the last, and soon, she was screaming as she felt the firestorm of her climax burn through her.

Osteus watched her and soon let out a roar of pleasure as he pulled her down deep on him and began to breed her. He sent a silent prayer to the great goddess of fertility and love as he slowly began to regain control over the satyr within him.

"You are the most exquisite creature that I have ever laid eyes on, my lamb. I love you more than there are stars in the skies above." Osteus said as he softly kissed her and then gently began to look over her body. "Was I too rough with you?"

Deyanira smiled and kissed him back. "No, my love. You were not. It seems the gods made me to be yours."

He gently set her down and helped her dress again before kissing her lovingly. He then dressed himself and gave a soft nod to the statue of the goddess.

She looked at the man's body. "Should we do something with him?" she asked softly.

Osteus shook his head. "No, he will become food for other creatures. Speaking of which, we should be heading home before they come out to feed. We have run into enough trouble for one evening." He said as he pulled out a torch from his pack and lit it before handing it to her. Deyanira knew that conversation was best saved for another time. She walked with him as he pulled the cart. It wasn't long before they were back at their quiet little home.

# 10
# HAPPINESS IN FATE
# AND MONSTROSITY

Summer had faded, and the changing of the leaves showed Persephone's descent back to her mate. Deyanira stepped out of the small hut carrying a tankard of warm cider for Osteus as he chopped wood for their home. On her heels was a small toddler who was one of their blessings. The half-mythic toddler ran up and bounced near his father in a pile of leaves.

"My love, take a break. Winter is not at our heels yet," she called to him as his ax swung down once more, splitting the large log.

Osteus looked at her and set down the ax before touching her pregnant belly. "By the Gods, you grow more beautiful with each passing day." He took the tankard and drank it down before giving a hearty laugh. "You spoil me. This is divine."

Deyanira smiled and kissed him. "I am just a blessed woman." She said as she watched their young one play.

He lifted her off the ground and kissed her deeply again. "We both are blessed," he said before putting her down. "How is our other sweet child treating you today?"

Deyanira smiled as she rubbed her belly. "Quite the little warrior like his...or her father." She said with a laugh.

Osteus looked at the house. "I am glad I finished the new room before Persephone's return. It won't be long before we will be calling the midwife." He said proudly.

"Whenever that happens, it will be a perfect day as always," she said happily. "Come now, Akakios. It is near sunset. It will be time for us to rest, and the other mythics will come out to play," she said, smiling as the toddler ran up and latched onto Osteus' leg.

Osteus had been an outcast most of his life, but these past few years with Deyanira showed him that he was everything to someone. He was not a monstrous beast to her. She had shown him he was worthy of love.

Deyanira's days were filled with love and passion as Osteus kept his promises to her. Though she was never able to return home, she had shown other neighboring villages that Osteus was a worthy ally, and many came to trust him.

Fate and monstrosity had brought them together, but in the end, they were happier than ever with their blessed family.

# ABOUT THE AUTHORS

## BRITTANY L. ADKINS

Brittany L. Adkins is a romance author who enjoys dipping her toes into all the subgenres of romantic fiction, including fantasy, horror, paranormal, contemporary, and erotic romance. Though she has an associate degree in massage therapy, she pursued her passion for writing and got her bachelor's degree in creative writing and fiction in 2016. She has always been an observer of people and culture, which has benefited her writing skills by allowing her to access knowledge of various cultures for depth in her characters and stories. This skill has always aided her in telling stories from multiple perspectives.

Many of her fellow writers have called her the Romantic Adventure Storyteller. She has also been mentored and created networking with writers in the entertainment and writing industry and the world of fandoms. She hopes her books will inspire an epidemic of reading.

Brittany is a podcaster who hosts two podcasts, Pagan's Witchy Corner and Pagan's Reading Nook. Both shows are available on your favorite podcast player. She is also a part-time blogger on Witchy Corner Productions. On her blog, you can find book reviews, articles about homesteading and paganism, and information on her books. She is also a landscape artist. Her art can also be found and purchased on her website.

Brittany lives in Tennessee on a small homestead with her husband, two children, and their dogs. She is also an MS warrior and enjoys reading, playing video games, and cosplaying in her free time.

Connect with her on social media.

Tiktok: @witchycornerproductions
Instagram: @witchycornerproductions
Website: www.witchycornerproductions.com

# J. T. BAXTER

J. T. Baxter was born in Leeds, England in the UK. At a young age he had a vivid imagination, and it was early in his childhood and into his teen years where he used writing to develop this.

Originally, he dabbled in fan fiction. Being a big fan of Star Trek, Star Wars, Marvel and DC, he used his imagination to write stories set in those universes.

In his teens and early twenties, J. T. moved into the realm of fantasy and began writing original stories within that genre.

Since meeting his writing partner, Brittany L. Adkins, J. T. is now concentrating more on the romance genre, particularly focusing on fantasy and erotic romances.

OTHER TITLES AVAILABLE FROM BRITTANY L. ADKINS

## FICTIONAL MUSINGS

Fictional Musings is a literary masterpiece that offers a dynamic range of creative manifestations. The author's transcendent tales are a mesmerizing experience, transporting you to worlds full of fantastic characters and circumstances. Death is no longer just a final curtain call, but a journey shrouded in mystery and wonder. The stories of unexpected romances between paranormal beings in forced proximity, and tales of intimacy will make the heart race. Accounts of secrets and forbidden passions will entice you into the grasp of irresistible danger, stirring a desire for more. Finally, the collection concludes with thought-provoking poems that explore the complexities of the soul, leaving an indelible impression. This spellbinding narrative guarantees that this mythical gem will invite you into the curiosities of love and shadow.

AVAILABLE AT YOUR FAVORITE BOOK RETAILER!

# WINNING JENN

The introduction to the corporate gods' "Poker Night" was anything but traditional for Jenn. A Mistake. An opportunity. Coercion. Control. Humiliation. Freedom? Each was a card in Jenn's hand. A game of chance that had become a game of power and fate. In this erotic tale, Jenn learns who holds the cards to her fate and it could be anyone's hand. The line between a winning bet and a losing hand is a fine one, and sometimes when they say "all in" they mean it.

NEW EXPANDED EDITION COMING SOON!

# COTTAGECORE READING AND REVIEW PLANNER

Love to read or share your favorite books? Want a fun way to track your literary journeys? Look no further than this fantastic reading and reviewing planner! I created this planner to keep track of my own reading adventures and blog reviews, but now I want to share it with all book lovers like you. It's packed with plenty of space for your notes and reflections on all your favorite reads. Let's make your reading journey unforgettable!

AVAILABLE ON AMAZON!

# HEARTH & SEED GARDEN PLANNER

A garden planner for all your planting adventures! This planner includes a companion planting section, a garden planning section listing all you want to grow, and a section to design where you want to plant everything. In addition to the garden planning sections, there is a harvest log and lots of space for notes.

I have also included one of my favorite blessings for the garden. Though I am pagan, this blessing can be used with any deity of your choice in any denomination.

May your garden flourish and bring you incredible abundance.

AVAILABLE ON AMAZON!

CHECK OUT THE PODCASTS!

# PAGAN'S WITCHY CORNER PODCAST

Welcome to Pagan's Witchy Corner! Here, you can find discussions on the world of witchcraft and the occult with some of the top voices in these communities. I will also share aspects of my own practice and how I integrate it into our life on our homestead. I also host guided meditations to broaden your personal practice.

# AVAILABLE ON YOUR FAVORITE PODCAST PLAYER!

# Pagan's Reading Nook Podcast

Welcome to my reading nook! Here, I will discuss the books I am reading, showcase new titles, and sit down with some amazing authors to talk about the worlds and characters they have created. We will discuss new releases, fan favorites, and classic tales that enchanted us. So grab your favorite hot or cold beverage and join me as we dive into the harrowing tales, seductive romances, and thrilling adventures of the fiction world.

# AVAILABLE ON YOUR FAVORITE PODCAST PLAYER!